'   was born and brought up in Harrow,

M   d as a painter at Hornsey Art School, and

lat   n at Harrow School of Art. She also spent

s   her, working with children with reading

        ow the well-known author/illustrator of

Rosi   *ears* and the *Bad Boris* books (Hutchinson).

        sie's first book for Frances Lincoln.

For Eloise Lily Maltby Maland,
with love – S. J-P.

First published in Great Britain in 1996 by
Frances Lincoln Limited, 4 Torriano Mews
Torriano Avenue, London NW5 2RZ

British Library Cataloguing in Publication Data
available on request.

ISBN 0-7112-1072-1 hardback
ISBN 0-7112-1083-7 paperback

Set in 22/26pt Plantin

Printed in Hong Kong

3 5 7 9 8 6 4 2

ANNIE ANGEL

Susie Jenkin-Pearce

FRANCES LINCOLN

Annie's grandma bought her angel wings for Christmas.

They were the best present of all.

Annie wore them all the time. She NEVER took them off!

"Annie's no angel," said Dad as he tucked her up in bed. "Only Grandma thinks so."

Annie wanted to wear her wings to school,
but Mum said, "No!" So Annie told Lucy
about her wings on the way.

The new topic at school was flight.
"We'll have a show at the end of term,"
said Miss Sally, their teacher.

"I have angel wings," said Annie. "Angels fly.
I could be an angel in the show."

"Mmm... How about being an aeroplane?"
smiled her teacher.

But Annie wanted to be an angel. She picked flowers for Miss Sally on the way to school.

She cleaned out the mouse.

She washed up the paint pots.

She tidied the books.

"Oh no, Annie!" gasped Miss Sally. "No more help, PLEASE."
Poor Annie. If only she did things right, like Lucy.

That night, Annie dreamed of angels.

She dreamed of flying about doing
kind things that DIDN'T go wrong.

But it was only a dream. Next morning, Annie carefully carried her wings to school.

"Lucy can wear these," she said. "She'll make the best angel."
"But Annie," said Miss Sally, "your wings were your special
present. Are you sure?"

Annie nodded and Miss Sally smiled.
"You wear them," she said. "Perhaps you'll
make a perfect angel after all."

And she did…

MORE PICTURE BOOKS IN PAPERBACK FROM FRANCES LINCOLN

ELLA AND THE RABBIT
Helen Cooper

Early one morning, Ella decides to visit her daddy's champion rabbit by herself.
Surely it wouldn't be naughty just to open the cage door a tiny crack...
A charming read-aloud picture book for the very young.

Nominated for the 1991 Kate Greenaway Medal
"Humorous, mischievous, true to life...a lovely book" *Nursery World*

ISBN 0-7112-0635-X

Suitable for National Curriculum English - Reading, Key Stage 1
Scottish Guidelines English Language - Reading, Level A

SHOUTING SHARON
David Pace

When Sharon shouts at the top of her voice, chaos ensues: 2 tired twins wake up and
howl, 4 fat ladies break their diets, and 9 brass bandsmen cause a riot. But one day
Sharon encounters 10 hungry lions, and suddenly she has met her match! A cautionary
counting tale with hilarious illustrations for parents and children to share.

ISBN 0-7112-0896-4

Suitable for National Curriculum English - Reading, Speaking and Listening, Key Stage 1
Scottish Guidelines English Language - Reading, Talking and Listening, Level A

ANIMAL PARADE
Jakki Wood

An exciting animal ABC featuring over 90 species parading nose-to-tail. With bright,
charming watercolours, this unusual alphabet book will delight every young reader.

ISBN 0-7112-0777-1

Suitable for National Curriculum English - Reading, Key Stage 1
Scottish Guidelines English Language - Reading, Level A

Frances Lincoln titles are available from all good bookshops.